Little Red Leaf

Beth W. Cardin

AuthorHouse™
1663 Liberty Drive
Bloomington, IN 47403
www.authorhouse.com
Phone: 1-800-839-8640

To, ~~██████████~~

I hope that your class enjoys my book!

~~██████████~~

First published by AuthorHouse 9/13/2010

ISBN: 978-1-4520-7414-6 (sc)

Library of Congress Control Number: 2010913696

Printed in the United States of America

This book is printed on acid-free paper.

authorHOUSE®

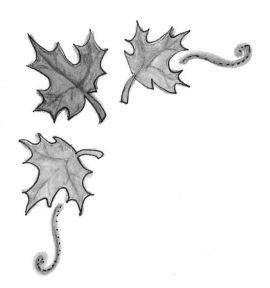

Look! Up here!! Near the top!!! I am the brightest, reddest leaf on this big, old maple tree! Look at me and all of my friends. We are magnificent! Look at all of the reds, yellows and oranges. Many people on the street below stop to see how beautiful we are. Sometimes they even take our picture! My life was great until.....

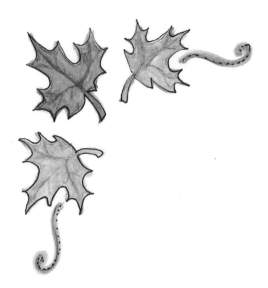

One day the wind started to blow. Then it blew a little harder and still a little harder. I was having a terrible time holding on to my branch. We were all being swirled around on our stems. I finally had to let go! It was terrifying!! What if I fell into a puddle and got all wet and mushy? Or what if I fell into the street and got squashed by a car? Help!!! I was really scared until.......

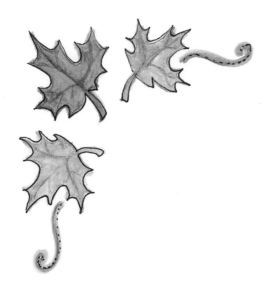

I fell with a soft thud onto something smooth and kind of slippery. It felt like I was still moving but I wasn't. I opened my eyes and looked straight into the eyes of a lady! I was on her windshield and we were driving down the street! I looked at her and she looked at me, so I tried to smile. I thought that I was OK until…......

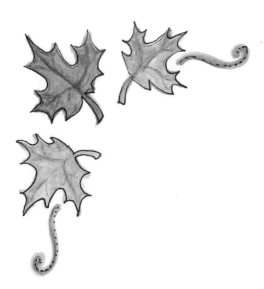

I saw her reach for the knob that turned the windshield wipers on. Yikes!!! I was going to get smooshed! What was I going to do? I was flat against the glass. I couldn't move! I thought that I was a goner until.......

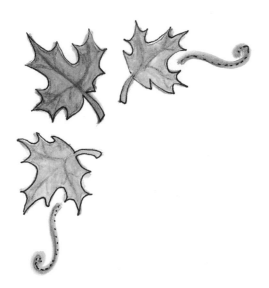

We took a corner and I shifted just a little bit. A breeze lifted me up just in time and off I went again! I was slip sliding along on that breeze wondering where in the world I would end up next. At least I was moving away from the street. Up and over a fence I went where I landed on some soft green grass. Whew!! I was getting so tired! I was thinking of taking a nice, long nap until.......

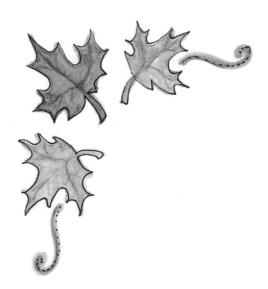

I heard the most HORRENDOUS noise! I looked all around and to my shocked surprise, I saw a man coming straight at me with a leaf blower. It was awful! All of the other leaves were being blown up into the air. Before I knew it I was being tossed all over. I didn't know which way was up or down! I thought that this was truly the end until......

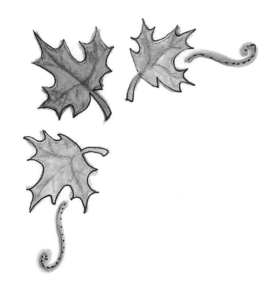

Suddenly, it was quiet. The man was gone. I found myself sitting on the top of a big pile of leaves. I was really tired but I was okay. Finally, I said to myself, I can try to get some rest. I closed my eyes and took a deep breath. I was about to fall asleep until.......

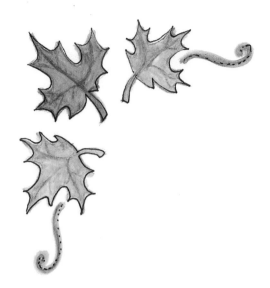

A little boy and a little girl came running around the corner. They were laughing and playing tag. I heard one of them say, "Hey, look at that big pile of leaves! What a great pile to jump in." I thought, JUMP IN?? Uh Oh! What do I do now? There wasn't even a whisper of a breeze to help me this time. I was ready to give up until......

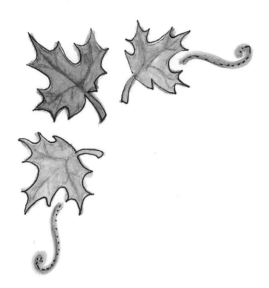

I was gently lifted into the little girl's hand and she said, "Look at this leaf. Why it's the brightest, reddest most beautiful leaf that I have ever seen! I am going to bring it home and put it into my scrapbook where it will last forever."

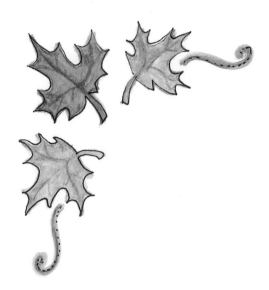

So, that is where I am today and I must say
that I look absolutely MAGNIFICENT!!!

CPSIA information can be obtained
at www.ICGtesting.com
Printed in the USA
LVIC07n2142230813
349427LV00001B

9 781452 074146